12$\frac{95}{}$

ISBN 8075-8692-7 LIBRARY OF CONGRESS CATALOG CARD 63-13332 © 1963 BY MIRIAM SCHLEIN
PUBLISHED SIMULTANEOUSLY IN CANADA BY GENERAL PUBLISHING, LIMITED, TORONTO
ALL RIGHTS RESERVED. PRINTED IN U.S.A.
15   14   13   12

ALBERT WHITMAN & COMPANY
NILES, ILLINOIS

THE WAY MOTHERS ARE

by MIRIAM SCHLEIN   pictures by JOE LASKER

Mother," said the little one,
swinging on a tree, "do you
love me?"

"Yes, I do," said the mother cat,
washing all the clothes.

"But Mother," said the little
one, "*why* do you love me when
sometimes I am naughty and run
away when you are trying to
dress me?"

"I never said I stopped loving you when you are naughty, did I?" asked his mother, hanging out the clothes.

"No," said the little one, "you didn't. But how can you love me when I scream and SCREAM, the way you don't like?"

I don't love you all the other time just because you are *not* screaming," said his mother. "So why should I stop loving you sometimes just because you *are* screaming?"

"I don't know," said the little one, scratching his head.

"But Mother, how can you really love me when sometimes I am naughty *all* day long, when I grab things away from sister, and knock her down, and throw my clothes all over the floor?"

"I can and do love you, even
those days," said his mother.
"Even though I don't really like
one single thing you do."

"But why?" said the little one.
"*Why* do you love me?"

"Why do you think?" asked
his mother.

The little one thought for a
minute and said, "You love me
because I am very smart and can
draw nice pictures!"

"You are smart, and you draw very
nice pictures. But that's not
why I love you," said his mother.

The little one thought some more,
as he held the dustpan for his
mother. Then he said, "I know.
You love me because some days I
am sweet to sister and let her
play with my blocks, my wagon,
all my toys, and I push her
gently in the swing!"

His mother said, "You make me happy when you do all those nice things. But that is not why I love you."

The little one thought and thought. Then he said, "I guess you love me then because so many days I eat what I should, and I brush my teeth and don't let the water splash all over the floor, and I sit very still in the car when we go someplace."

he little one took a deep breath. "And, those days, I put my toys away, and go to bed when I'm supposed to, too.

That's why you love me," he said— this time very certain—"because lots of days I am so good."

"It's awfully nice on those days
when you are really so good,"
said his mother, sitting down
at last. "But even that is not
the reason I love you."

"Then why?" said the little one,
and he took a flying leap and
landed on his mother's lap.
"Why *do* you love me?"

"I love you," she answered,
"because you are *my* little one,
my very own child.

From the moment you were born
I cared for you, and wanted
what was best for you.

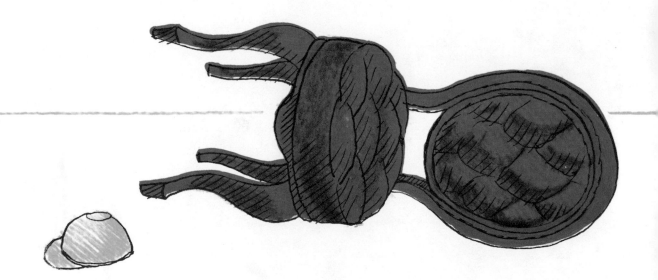

So you
don't think I love you just when
you're good, and stop loving you
when you are naughty, do you?
That's not the way mothers are.
I love you all the time, because
you are mine."

"Is that the reason?" asked the
little one. "That's so simple!"

"Yes," said the mother, giving
him a big tight hug. "That's the
reason. And it is so simple.
But that's the way mothers are."

"I'm glad that's the way mothers
are!" said the little one.
And he hugged her right back,
very tight.